Mirandi Riwoe is a Brisbane-based writer. She has been shortlisted for the *Overland* Neilma Sidney Short Story Prize, the Josephine Ulrick Short Story Prize and the Luke Bitmead Bursary. She has also been longlisted for the *ABR* Elizabeth Jolley Short Story Prize and CWA (UK) dagger awards. Her work has appeared in *Review of Australian Fiction, Rex, Peril* and *Shibboleth and Other Stories*. Her first novel, *She be Damned*, will be released by Legend Press (UK) and Pantera (Aus) in 2017. Mirandi has a PhD in Creative Writing and Literary Studies (QUT).

the Fish girl

Mirandi Riwoe

First published in Seizure by Xoum in 2017

Xoum Publishing
PO Box Q324, QVB Post Office,
NSW 1230, Australia

www.seizureonline.com
www.xoum.com.au

Text copyright © Mirandi Riwoe 2017

This work is copyright. Apart from any use as permitted under the *Copyright Act 1968*, no part of this publication may be reproduced, stored in or introduced into a retrieval system, or transmitted in any form or by any means (electronic, mechanical, photocopying, recording or otherwise), without the prior written permission of the publisher.

The moral right of the author has been asserted.

Grateful acknowledgement is made for permission to quote the extracts on pages 1, 29 and 81. © Somerset Maugham Estate.

ISBN 978-1-925589-06-1 (print)
ISBN 978-1-925589-07-8 (digital)

Cataloguing-in-publication data is available from the National Library of Australia

Internal design and typesetting © Xoum Publishing 2017

Cover illustration and design by Sam Paine, www.sampaine.com
Printed in Australia by Lightning Source

Edited by Alice Grundy

Viva la Novella V was made possible through the generous support of Xoum Publishing.

For Ellen, woman of my heart

One of these days he would buy himself a house on the hills in Java and marry a pretty little Javanese. They were so small and so gentle and they made no noise, and he would dress her in silk sarongs and give her gold chains to wear round her neck and gold bangles to put on her arms.

W. Somerset Maugham,
The Four Dutchmen

I

In the darkness before dawn the village men row out in their boats that are shaped like the half-pods from the criollo tree, and in the heat of the day the women scale, clean and smoke the fish the men bring home.

When Junius comes from town in search of cheap labour for the Dutch Resident's kitchen, he calls out to the villagers in their Sunda dialect.

An older, leathery fisherman steps forward. 'My daughter is good with the scaling knife.' His voice grates, as if a fish bone jags his throat.

'How old is she?' Junius asks.

The fisherman stares at him for a few moments and then shakes his head. 'She comes to here,' he says, holding his fingers level with the bottom of his earlobe.

Junius's eyebrow lifts. Although he has only a quarter Dutch blood, he is paler than the crowd of under-dressed men before him, and knows how to wear trousers and a necktie. 'Bring her to me. I'll have to look at her first.'

The fisherman disappears in search of his daughter, while the others press the virtues of their family members on the man from town. Two women, still clutching the baskets they are weaving, babies nestled close to their chests in batik *slendangs*, cry out to him, urge him to take their older daughters. A group of men approaches from the beach, tying their sarongs tight about their hips, bare feet shuffling along the sandy earth. Some of them ignore Junius, return to their shacks clustered in neat rows behind the ceremonial hut, but three younger ones stay on, push to the front of the crowd.

Soon the older fisherman returns, followed by a slight girl, her midriff and legs wrapped in a roughly woven sarong. Her straight hair hangs over her face so that only a glimpse of her eyes and nose is visible. Her feet are bare and her shoulders, rounded forward, accentuate her small, pubescent breasts.

She is jostled on either side by young men and

women, hopeful to gain work in the Dutch quarters. The young men call out to Junius, grinning and joking, but the girl keeps her head bowed.

Junius nods to one lean man and then another, gesturing for them to join him, before stopping in front of the girl. 'Pull your hair back.'

The girl, eyes still trained upon the ground, parts her hair with the backs of her hands, so that the shiny tresses arc like the wings of a black bird.

'What is her name?' Junius asks the fisherman.

'Mina.'

Junius's eyes linger on her high cheekbones and fine mouth and he nods. 'She will do. Have her ready to leave in the morning.'

A sob of dismay rises in the girl's chest but lodges in her throat like a frog in a tree hollow, for she knows better than to cry out. She has never roamed far from the edges of the tiny village, no further than a few metres into the forest that backs onto the beach. Even when the other children disappear deep into the shadowy folds of the casuarina trees to play, she stays behind to help her mother sweep the house or scrape the fish. How will she bear to be so far away from everything she knows?

Following her father the short distance to their home, she keeps her face lowered, away from the gaze of curious villagers. They reach their hut, elevated on short stilts, the walls a medley of bark and timber with a shaggy, thatched roof. Her mother is standing on the narrow landing.

'What have you done?' she asks, her chapped fingers clutching at her sarong. Her eyes switch from her husband to her daughter and then back to her husband. 'What have you done?'

The old fisherman simply stares at his wife. His eyes are bloodshot — are always bloodshot — as if the glittering sun has saturated him with its heat. He eventually shrugs past her into the darkness of the hut.

Mina doesn't enter as there is only the one room. She can already hear her mother's voice, soft and plaintive, working at her father, and his low grunts in response. They very rarely exchange harsh words, the last time being two years before when her father wanted Mina to wed. Her mother succeeded in dissuading him then, saying she was too young. Would she succeed this time?

Mina walks down to the beach and contemplates the small triangles of silver fish arrayed on the nets. Her mother has laid them out to dry but it is becoming dark, so Mina wraps them in spare netting and pulls the lot up to the side of the hut, away from night-time predators. She knows that tomorrow there will be more fish, damp and fleshy, ready to be scaled and gutted. And that the next day there will be even more. She stares at her feet, at the sand and strands of grass, and for the first time feels a flicker of curiosity. What will be expected of her at the Dutch house? More fish?

Standing at the corner of the hut, next to a cluster of freshly salted sardines strung to the end of a rod, she listens for her parents, but all is quiet now. Her father comes out and sits on the end of the landing and lights a *rokok*, the aura of clove and tobacco smoke rising above his head. A metallic clatter of cooking echoes out from the back and she joins her mother at the fire. She's frying chilli and fish paste and despite herself, Mina feels hunger stir in her stomach. She squats down and begins to break apart some salted fish to add to the pot.

'Do I have to go?' she asks.

Her mother wipes the side of her nose with the heel of her hand as if to brush away tears, although she's not crying. She nods. 'Yes.'

'But why? Have I done wrong?'

There are creases between the older woman's brows from when she frowns against the glare of the sun and privation. These lines have become deeper with time, and now resemble keen, inch-long slices in her forehead. She shakes her head, chopping *kangkung* to add to the fish. 'No. No, it's not that, Tak-tak.' Mina knows she's not in trouble when her mother uses her nickname, starfish. Her mother tosses the greens into the pan and stirs them about, and then wipes sweat from her upper lip. 'Your father thinks you will be better off there. You can work, and maybe even send us things sometimes.'

'What things?'

Her mother shrugs. 'Food? Maybe clothing.'

'But how?'

'Your father says you will exchange your hours of work for things we need, like more spice and tobacco.'

'But how will I do this?'

'I am not sure,' her mother answers, shaking her head slowly. 'Your father thinks your Dutch master will allow you to visit us once in a while, so maybe then you could bring us back some goods.'

Mina rests back onto her haunches, and sniffs at the salty fish crumbled against her fingers. 'What work will I do there?'

'What you do here, I expect. Cooking, sweeping, washing.' Her strong, bony hand squeezes Mina's knee. 'But you must behave yourself. Remember where you come from. Remember your father and me. Remember one day you must return to us, Tak-tak.' Her voice is quivering now, and Mina feels the force of tears against the back of her eyes. 'And never let anyone see this,' her mother adds, folding back a corner of the girl's sarong.

They stare at the scaly, red rash that covers her inner thighs.

Mina swiftly re-covers her mottled skin, conscious of the fire's heat upon the weeping sores.

—

The three of them have their meal seated around the fire. They eat the rice and fish from banana leaves with their fingers, and Mina asks, licking the seasoning from her shiny fingertips, 'What will I eat there?'

'Food,' her mother says.

'Yes, but what kind of food? Will it be the same as here?'

Her mother glances at her father, and she knows her mother is trying to gauge how long until he loses his temper and slopes off to smoke. 'I'm not sure, Tak-tak. Shh, now.'

And what will she wear? What is the town like? Who will she work with? She asks herself these questions, a tremor of excitement finally mingling with the dread in her stomach, making her feel pleasantly sick like when she eats too much *sirsak*, the sweetness of the custard apple curdling in her stomach.

The evening sun sets as they clear away the pots, food and drying fish, and they retire to their rattan mats in the hut. Mina wonders where she will sleep in the Dutch house. She has only ever seen a white man once. He was tall, as willowy as a kanari sapling, and he wore strange clothes like the man from town. He'd trod through their village, peering into their huts, as curious as the villagers were as they gazed upon him.

Through a gap in the wall next to where she sleeps, Mina watches the swaying, frayed leaves of the coconut trees on the beach. The waves roll and clap further out to sea, and she hears the familiar hum of the ocean calling to her. Her father snores softly, but she knows her mother is lying awake too.

—

There is a damp breeze from the water as the sun rises. Mina's father strides onto the beach and glares out at the fishing boats already bobbing on the waves, fidgeting old netting between his hands. Moving back to the landing, he cracks pumpkin seeds between his teeth, making a slight whooshing sound with his lips as he spits the shells to the ground. Her mother stirs coconut milk and palm sugar into Mina's breakfast rice, a sure treat, but Mina is afraid again and almost unable to eat. She forces the meal down, gagging, determined to not waste the food that her mother would never allow herself. Finally she stands and her mother carefully wraps her own good sarong around her daughter's hips. The patterned batik is still stiff from the wax stamping, the colours earthy, with streaks of ocean blue. Mina tries to protest, for this is her mother's special sarong for ceremonial days, but the older woman clicks her tongue and ignores her. They are both weeping now, as her mother tucks and pats down the edges of the fabric, and tucks a little more, until her father grumbles that it is time to go.

Mina trails behind her father to the centre of the village, wiping snot and tears onto the back of her hand. When her father leaves her with Junius, the man from town, he squeezes her upper arm — reassuring or cautioning, she's not sure. He doesn't look at her. He glances above her head for a few moments, as if contemplating the branches of the mango trees, and then turns and leaves. She watches his sinewy, dark legs from behind and she feels a fissure of hatred for him. Fear slices through her anger. Oh, the gods will have something terrible in store for her for thinking such things.

'I hope you have eaten and drunk well this

morning,' says Junius, as he swings up onto his pony. 'It's a long walk to Wijnkoopsbaai.'

There are two brown ponies. One is fat and carries Junius's gear on one side of its saddle and two baskets of fish on the other. Junius's own pony is taller, yet his feet dangle only a foot from the ground as he sways along. Mina falls in behind the two young men — Yati and Ajat. Yati is short, as squat as an eggplant, but Ajat, one of the chief's sons, stands tall, has the broad shoulders and trim waist of a fine fisherman. They walk slowly from the village. A few friends clap the men on the shoulders, grinning, demanding they bring back some cinnamon or nutmeg. One even calls for them to bring back prospective wives, and he's slapped playfully across the top of the head by his companions. It becomes awkward, for the young men don't know when to stop their cajoling, when to stop following, but finally Junius frowns down upon them and they pause under the fragrant kenanga tree that marks the edge of the village. After a few seconds one of the young men left behind calls out to his friends to bring back a *peci* to replace his straw hat, but the ribaldry is done with.

The first part of their journey is pleasant enough as they walk in the shade of row upon row of India rubber trees. The sun is still low and not yet punishing, and the ground is damp and cool. But by mid-morning the girl, who is not used to such long periods of trudging, is weary and hot. She sees glistening perspiration ring the necklines of the young men ahead of her, and her mother's sarong is damp around her waist. The mountainous terrain becomes dusty, the straggle of bushes offering little shade. Her feet are sore, and the tip of her right big toe bleeds from where she jabbed it on a rock. By the time they reach Wijnkoopsbaai she is wilting, her skin greasy with sweat.

Here the roads are wider, no longer single tracks, arcing a path through a verdant patchwork of tea plantations. Small houses, square and neat with sloped roofs, line the roads next to large plots of rice paddies. Clothing is cast over shrubs to dry, and children and chickens watch them as they walk past. Mina marvels at the never-ending stream of houses.

They come to a crossroad, where the boulevard widens, leading down to the seafront. Oxen laden with baskets plod past white men on horseback. Junius pulls his pony up in front of a gate at the top of the road, and a boy runs out to open the latch. The girl stands on tip-toe but cannot see over the orderly hedges that surround the property. She is the last through, lagging behind the others. She can't resist staring at the creamy orchids or reaching for a fallen *bunga raya*, its happy red petals having narrowly escaped the heavy tread of the ponies. The road is steep but finally they see the house. It's much larger than even the ceremonial hut back in the village. It is stark white, with timber shutters, columns and wrought iron balustrades. Even Yati and Ajat are struck dumb by its majesty.

Junius hustles them around to the back of the house. Kneeling in the shade of a frangipani tree are two kitchen maids, dark and slim, grinding seeds in a mortar and pestle. They lean into each other and watch as the young men from the village take water from a pail. The maids each wear plain white *kebayas* over matching brown and black sarongs, and have their shiny black hair pulled into low ponytails. They look so smart Mina is glad she's wearing her mother's good sarong after all.

Once the soggy baskets of fish are unloaded from the horses, Junius tells her to stay in the courtyard until she is collected, and he leads the village men and ponies away to the stables. Her legs feel heavy so she squats down onto her haunches, and watches the servant girls go about their work. They finish with the seeds, and start slicing chillies and lemongrass on a wooden board on the ground before them. They talk to each other, but they do not talk to her. One of them rises to lug the heavy baskets up the back stairs to the kitchen verandah, her back arched with the weight of the fish.

An older woman comes from the kitchen to inspect the fish and, noticing Mina, descends the stairs with crablike steps to allow for the girth of her stomach. She stands in front of the girl and looks her over, like she is a piece of fruit at the market. She makes Mina turn, and even squeezes her upper arms, feeling for muscle tone.

'You will call me Ibu Tana,' the woman says. 'I am the master's head cook. You will work for me in the kitchen, but if you are no good, you will have to be one of the cleaning maids. Do you understand?'

Ibu Tana is shorter than Mina. Her hair, black with wires of grey sprouting at the hairline, is pulled into a severe bun, and her skin is saggy and lumpy. She reminds Mina of a toad.

'Do you understand?' the cook repeats. 'Pray to the gods, they didn't send me someone who doesn't speak the language, did they?' she then says, exasperated, to the other kitchen maids.

Mina nods. 'I understand.' Her mother was born in a village on the outskirts of Wijnkoopsbaai where this language of trade was used often. As they knelt in the shallows together, scooping the muck and worm-like innards from the fish, she'd taught Mina many of these words, and told her of bold women like this Ibu Tana.

The cook wraps her steel fingers around Mina's arm again and pulls her to a hut at the back of the courtyard. Inside is the servants' *mandi*, the tub filled with clean water. Ibu Tana grasps the end of Mina's sarong and unravels it from her body, her gnarled fingers rasping the girl's skin. Mina covers the rash on her thighs with her hands, but Ibu Tana pushes her towards the *mandi* and tells her to wash with the sandalwood oil, to change into the servant's sarong and *kebaya* neatly folded next to the wash bucket. The *mandi* door slams shut behind her. Mina has never washed like this before, for a modest sunset soak in the sea is considered ample cleansing in the village. She picks up the small bucket by the *mandi* and dips it in the water. Lifting the bucket above her head she lets the cool water sluice over her body. She repeats this three times, until she is shivering.

Looking around, she can't find anything to dry herself with. Ibu Tana has taken her mother's sarong and all that is left are the servant clothes. She feels a flutter of panic; she doesn't want to keep Ibu Tana waiting. Quickly she wraps the new sarong around her wet hips. It is the same as those worn by the other servant girls. The pattern is far fancier than any she has ever seen before; a shower of black tadpoles in symmetrical russet swirls. The *kebaya* feels strange as she gingerly pokes her hands into the sleeves and pulls the blouse onto her body, for she's not used to the feel of fabric against her back, rubbing against her shoulders and breasts. She's not sure how she'll ever become used to the confinement.

She climbs the back steps to the kitchen slowly, but once there, her trepidation turns to amazement as she gazes around the huge room at the number of stoves and pots. She's never seen an oven built into a fireplace before. There are glass-front cabinets, bowls and plates stacked high. One of the kitchen maids is washing crockery in a large tub while the other one stands in front of a bubbling pot of oil. A houseboy pauses in his sweeping and grins at her.

Ibu Tana turns from the oven to look at her. A slow smile curls the side of her mouth. 'The fish girl has brought the smell of the sea with her,' she says. 'You'd better be careful or we'll accidentally fry you up with the crabs.'

The kitchen maids titter when Mina bends her head to sniff her arm, but Ibu Tana shakes her head and tells her to shell the beans.

Ibu Tana tries to teach her to cook other dishes besides fried fish with sambal. The cook grumbles that nobody can live on fried fish alone. Of course, Mina knows this to be untrue. She is aghast at the variety of food the master and his guests insist upon, that even the servants enjoy. Only on very special occasions is a chicken or goat slaughtered in her village. And only the men eat their fill; women and children busily clear the cooking pots, douse the fire, sweep the hearth while waiting for what rice or meat might remain. But in the Dutch house Mina eats well, tastes sauces and sweets she never knew existed. She wishes her mother could try these wonderments, and vows to take her some food wrapped in banana leaves when she returns to the village for a visit, even if she has to steal morsels from behind Ibu Tana's back.

One of the first things she learns to cook is *pisang epe*. Ibu Tana teaches her to fry the banana with palm sugar until it is brittle and sweet, how to recognise when to take it from the pan. Mina learns to knead dough for Dutch desserts and Chinese dumplings, how to slice the shallots and garlic so finely that, when fried, they become as wispy as wood shavings.

Once the day's cooking has been done and all the dishes washed and sorted, Mina stands on the kitchen balcony and breathes in the traces of spice left on her fingertips — the peppery coriander, the tang of the lime leaves. She smells the night air, searching for the salt of the sea on the evening breeze. She closes her eyes and strains to hear the ocean's whisper, which is occasionally disrupted by a dog barking or the night call of an owl. It's in these closing moments of each night, when she feels the ocean's presence, Mina remembers who she is. But the memory has weight, sinks in her chest like a pebble in the sea. She misses her mother. She misses the silence of plaiting the netting with her, she misses their rhythm of scaling the fish. She misses falling asleep besides her mother's soft breathing, while the ocean whispers to her through the gap in the wall.

Each night at the Dutch house the kitchen maids sleep on bamboo mats on the kitchen floor. If the room is stuffy from the day's cooking and the others are already quietly snoring, Mina pulls her mat outside onto the verandah and braves the mosquitos by hiding under her mother's sarong. The morning after she had arrived at the master's house she was horrified to see the sarong cast on the ground, bunches of washed spinach arranged in rows upon it. She was too scared to say anything. All day she waited and watched between the tasks Ibu Tana had set for her. She waited until the kitchen maids cleared away the greens, their bare, flat feet treading across the sarong as they went. Then Mina flicked the sarong into her grasp, rolled it into a ball, hid it away under a bush until nightfall. That first night when she brought it out from its hiding place, when she lay with the sarong across her mat, her skin cringed, waiting for Ibu Tana's sharp words, a clip to the ear. But nothing happened. Maybe they didn't notice. Maybe they didn't care.

—

Although she works alongside the other two kitchen maids in the small, hot kitchen every day, they are locked together in their own dialect and their own history, for they are sisters come all the way from Aceh. The houseboy is friendlier, younger, so young he still doesn't have any down on his cheeks, or across his upper lip. His name is Pepen and he's small with a thin face and ears that stick out from his head. He has been with the master for so long he can barely remember his parents and doesn't know what village he is from. All he has left from that time is a small *kris*, fastened to his waist, its wavy, sharp blade sheathed in leather.

The first story Pepen ever tells her, while they

roast cacao beans over the fire, is how he watched a man in the market have a fit; how the man just collapsed to the ground and shivered, how his spit frothed like waves on a windy day.

'And there was this terrible smell. It seemed to seep from his skin, a frightened smell, a rotten smell,' he says. 'And he swallowed his tongue.' Pepen blinks a few times, and the tips of his large ears become red.

Pepen's job is to sweep the floors and polish the timber, fill the *mandis* and bring in wood for the fires. Sometimes, when Ibu Tana gets irritated and shoves her aside, Mina helps Pepen with his chores. One morning she follows him into the dining room, for she'd spilt the cooking fat, been banished from the kitchen. The main section of the house is vast and airy. Palm fronds nod in the dulcet breeze that drifts through the open doors, and the heavy furniture from the master's homeland seems to overwhelm the delicate teak pieces.

She's sweeping the floor, the spidery straw of the broom wafting ash and dust against her ankles, when she notices Ajat, one of the young men who'd accompanied her from the fishing village, standing in the doorway.

'What are you doing?' She doesn't know him very well. Growing up, her shyness had bound her close to her mother and home, and she'd always been extra bashful of Ajat, the son of the head fisherman. But she yearns to feel the language of their village upon her tongue, wants to feel she is still a part of something.

'Waiting for Master,' he says. His skin is as smooth as polished ebony, dark and tight, and his wiry hair is tucked into a batik headwrap. 'I've brought his horse.'

He doesn't offer any more information, just stands patiently on his right foot, the other one tucked against his right ankle. Mina resumes her sweeping but feels his eyes upon her and becomes self-conscious, all elbows and shuffling feet. She doesn't notice the master of the house enter the room upon a cloud of tobacco smoke.

'Be more careful, girl,' he snaps at her, as he squashes the cigarette beneath his shoe. He watches Mina for a few moments through his pale crow's eyes and then says, his tone less harsh, 'You're making more mess than there was before.' He walks onto the verandah and leans over the rail to the pond. Bringing up the phlegm in his throat, he hocks into its green depths.

Mina sees Ajat's mouth twitch as she sweeps the ash towards the corner of the room. She's forgotten to bring the dustpan with her and is unsure what to do with the debris. Conscious of Ajat's gaze, she tucks the broom under her arm and returns to the back of the house in search of Pepen.

—

'What do you mean he wants the fish girl to serve?' demands Ibu Tana. 'She can barely hold a pot without spilling *lodeh* down her front.'

It's true. The girl fingers the stiff yellowish soup stain that has dried upon her *kebaya*. She thinks she will never become used to the cook's abrupt ways. It's as though her hands aren't her own when Ibu Tana is near and her heart jitters high in her throat. Sometimes when Ibu Tana scolds, a crystalline blind spot nudges at the corner of her vision.

Pepen shrugs. 'The master said he wants her to wait table from now on. He said when she's not working for you during the day, she is to help me in the house.'

Ibu Tana stares at the girl for a moment, her mouth twisted to the side, eyes narrowed. 'Well, you'd better change your *kebaya*.' She reaches out, pinching the fabric between her fingers, catching the tiniest bit of flesh.

—

Later that day Mina returns a spittoon to the sitting room. She pauses, hearing Ibu Tana's voice, high-pitched. She hides behind the doorway, for she doesn't want to anger the cook.

'She has leprosy, I tell you,' Ibu Tana is saying. 'I've seen it. It's disgusting.'

Penyakit kusta. Leprosy. The girl's hand twitches at her sarong and she feels her ears burn red. Was Ibu Tana talking about her? Please don't let it be so. Her family had taken much care over the years to hide the offensive flesh. Who knew what the other village families would have done to her if they thought she could contaminate them too? And her father had traded much fish and shells for herbs to alleviate the itchiness, the pain. But somehow she'd been careless enough for Ibu Tana to notice.

'Rubbish.' The master's voice is low and clipped. 'It would be obvious if she had this sickness.'

'But she does,' the cook insists. 'I have seen it myself upon her legs. What if she passes it to all of us? What then? It would not be good if it is known that this sickness is in the house. Who will visit you then?'

'That is my concern, not yours.' Mina hears him strike a match to light his cigarette. 'Bring her to me.'

It doesn't occur to the girl to run, she has been brought up to be obedient, after all. Ibu Tana almost collides with her as she bustles around the corner and grabs her by the arm. 'Were you listening, you sly thing?'

The girl nods. Her face is hot as she's dragged to the master, worse than on the day her father gave her to Junius. She won't look up at him, just stares at his richly polished brogues.

'Show me your legs, girl,' he says. His tone is abrupt, but softens when he repeats, 'Show me your legs. There's nothing to be scared of. Ibu Tana is here. We just want to be certain you are not sickly.'

Her breath won't come as she slowly parts her sarong at the front. Averting her face to the left, Mina squeezes her eyes shut and can almost feel her skin bloom fresh red welts under the others' gaze.

'That is nothing more than a rash, you foolish woman,' the master says eventually.

'You won't send her away?' asks Ibu Tana.

The girl's eyes lift to meet the master's. She would walk into the sea rather than disgrace her father. Her mother.

'Of course not.'

Mina can't sleep listening to Ibu Tana's cranky snore. Any wariness she felt for the woman has been replaced with a sullen dislike, as unyielding as the twin shells of a fresh clam. Just the memory of her words to the master pulses heat through the girl's body, making the sores on her thighs flare and sting. She wants to rake her fingernails through the welts, really dig at the itch, but knows the lacerating damage is not worth the momentary relief.

If she were at home her mother would soak cabbage leaves, drape them over the sores. She would mash papaya, chew betel nut, smear the paste across the rash. But here, in Ibu Tana's kitchen, the girl lies in agony, too embarrassed to tend to the sores. If she were home in her village she would wade into the water, let its salt balm the pain. The warm water would lap at her legs, dissipate the burn.

Mina longs to hear the ocean but cannot over the others' sleeping breaths. Tip-toeing onto the verandah, she leans over the railing, but can only hear the lowest murmur from the sea. She wants it to be louder, loud enough to drown out the high pitch of pain that hums through her body. She steals down the steps, across the master's land, until she reaches the gate. It's locked, so she scrambles through the hedges, the branches snagging her *kebaya*, scratching her arms, until she reaches the road. The clammy sea breeze draws her forth, and she's not afraid when there's a rustle in the bushes and a gecko clucks from inside a tree trunk, for her need to be in the ocean clamours through her body. She ignores the rocks and prickles that pierce the soft soles of her feet, the burrs that cling to the bottom of her sarong.

Thin reeds whip her shins as she runs onto the beach, the sand still warm from the heat of the day. The full moon shines across the slate surface of the sea. The waves rush up the wet sand towards her, their frothy white fingers greedily beckoning to her as they retreat. She sheds her sarong and clambers into the cool water. Sinks to her knees. Feels a flash of pain as the water licks at the sores on her thighs, but then, the relief. A sigh catches in her throat as she leans back, digging her palms into the sand behind her. She lengthens her legs, and the salt water lolls against her tortured skin. Her whole body gently rolls back and forth with the rhythm of the sea.

She stands and steps a few feet further into the water. She's careful because she's never learnt to swim. Too many of their village men and children had drowned for Mina to be careless. But the sea pulls her further until the chill water reaches her hips. The current is strong, tugging at her body so that she sways on the spot, and her feet seep into the sand. The sea's roar, hollow, familiar, rushes through her, talks to her, matches its cadence to hers. It reaches around her, velvet soft, draws her in, draws her further until the water is at her waist. Its arms are so soft, softer than the white underbelly of the stingray, and she can hear it whispering to her. *Putri*. Princess. *Putri*. Its arms are dark and long, gently sucking, kissing at her damaged skin, until the agony of flesh melts away, leaving a faint tingle in its place.

Mina shivers, for a breeze has picked up. She backs out of the water and, once on the beach again, drops into a low curtsy, murmurs her thanks to Nyai Loro Kidul, apologises that she didn't bring a flower or shell as an offering. She feels heavy, restful. She's so relaxed she could fall asleep on the sand, but knows that the Ocean Queen cannot protect her there, so she slips back to the hot kitchen, back to her bamboo mat.

The captain was always losing his head over one
brazen hussy after another . . .

W. Somerset Maugham,
The Four Dutchmen

II

Mina wonders if envy, as redolent as soured durian, makes Ibu Tana hiss at her through her remaining teeth. For Ibu Tana the girl seems to have become a favourite of the master's. She has freedoms the older woman has never experienced. When she isn't in the kitchen being bossed around by the head cook, she can be found in the cool, relaxed world of the main house and the steamy, harried kitchen. Maybe, too, Ibu Tana resents how the master calls for Mina with the word *mooi*, which means 'beautiful' in his language.

Mina helps Pepen return some bedding to the spare room and catches a glimpse of herself in the mirror. She's seen the shape of her thighs, her buttocks, when reflected in the puddle upon the *mandi* floor. She's seen the shadow of herself in the still water of the well, in the window panes of the master's house. But never like this. Her fingers trace her full bottom lip. She leans in close to the mirror so she can search out the flecks in the brown irises, the curl in her lashes. She smiles. So this is *mooi*. She doesn't linger long at the mirror, for Pepen is grinning at her.

'The master's sister stayed in this room when she visited from Belanda,' he says, sweeping under the mahogany four-poster bed. He straightens and the grin slips from his face. 'She was bitten by a mosquito and her foot swelled up so she couldn't put her shoes on for many days. Her doctor — one of their doctors, they would not see the medicine man Ibu Tana sends for — wanted to saw her foot off but the master wouldn't let him.' He shrugs. 'Luckily she got her feet back into her slippers and she returned home to Belanda. The master was very sad.'

—

Back in the kitchen Mina squeezes the juice from a grapefruit, wondering how the master can stand the sour fruit. She thinks of the sweet, green mandarins that grow near her village, and kisses her tongue against the roof of her mouth until she can almost taste their juice.

'Fish girl,' says Ibu Tana, shoving a piece of clothing over Mina's shoulder. 'The master wants you to fetch goods from the produce store. You're to change into this.'

The girl holds the *kebaya* up before herself. The front panels of the silk blouse reach her ankles; the cloth's rosy lustre is like nothing she has ever seen before. She's confused as to what she's supposed to do but Ibu Tana has already gone. She looks to the kitchen maids, who pretend to ignore her, even though they peer at her from under their heavy brows as they fry and chop the evening's meal.

The *kebaya* is heavy on her shoulders as she waits on the kitchen verandah for further instructions. Its fabric is thick. It blocks the sea breeze. But it's gorgeous, and she can't help running her palms down her sides, her work-roughened skin catching on the silk.

She's pleasantly surprised when Ajat guides the pony and cart to the back steps. She's glad that he will see her in her finery.

'Come along,' he calls to her. 'I'm to take you to the store.'

'But I don't know what we need to get,' she

protests, looking through the kitchen door in vain for Ibu Tana.

'I have the list,' Ajat says. 'I'm to help load the goods, you're to make sure that sneaky Chinaman doesn't swindle the master.'

She struggles to climb the steep steps of the buggy due to the tightness of her sarong. Once there Ajat shifts over on the bench seat to make room for her. She takes the chalkboard from him, stares at the calligraphy scrawled across its surface.

'We can't read this.'

Ajat grins. 'The Chinaman doesn't know that.'

They're quiet on the short drive to the produce store. Her arm rubs against his as they sway along the dirt road and she watches for finches in the trees, on the curiously shaped roofs of the Dutch houses. Sometimes she glances down at Ajat's fingers, dark and tapered, controlling the reins. She peers at the vein that ropes up from the heel of his hand and across his forearm. He doesn't smell of the sea anymore. His scent is sweeter, of sweat and horse. His knee bumps against hers once in a while.

They trundle down the road towards the beach and she leans forward, yearning for a touch of the salt water on her toes.

Ajat presses her back. 'No swimming today,' he says. 'Junius needs the cart again soon.'

He pulls the buggy alongside a square building. Mina stares at the sloped red roof. At the peak of each eave is a golden creature, scrolled and lizard-like.

'Dragons,' a voice says from behind. 'They are called dragons. They guard my store.'

The Chinese merchant holds his hand up to her, takes the chalkboard, looks it over. He's shorter than Ajat, but much more stout. His head is the shape of a pumpkin, and his sparse black hair is slicked to his pate with perspiration. He grunts at the list and gestures for them to follow him into the back of the store.

The space is filled with such an assortment of produce Mina can only stare. Bolts of fabric, sacks of rice and tapioca, greens, fruit and dried sea-cucumber among chests of crockery, baskets of silk slippers, fans and seeds. She doesn't recognise many of the goods with their strange scents, awkward shapes. Two young women stand behind a counter. They resemble the Chinese merchant; wide faces, shiny black hair. They wear heavy smocks with long sleeves and pretty buttons. Gold bangles jangle up and down their arms and jade earrings dangle from their ears. One is trying to catch a striped *gurami* from the aquarium behind her, although the fish sluggishly bobs away from her net. The other woman stares back until Mina drops her gaze and returns to the hot yard.

Ajat helps the merchant's men fill the cart with sacks of food. Lastly, they heft up a wooden barrel.

'Beer,' says Ajat. 'Junius says that the master doesn't drink it, but he has guests coming tonight who drink a lot.'

—

The afternoon sun has lost its heat and myna birds argue among the branches, dropping shreds of leaf onto the patio. Mina is crouched down grinding dried coriander seeds in the stone mortar. The crushed coriander resembles silt, she thinks, as she dips the tip of her finger into it, rubs its chalkiness between her finger and thumb. She touches her fingers to her nose, against the surface between her nostrils, so she can smell its sharp fragrance. Pepen half-heartedly sweeps away the fallen leaves of the persimmon trees nearby while telling her of the cargo tramp that arrives in port most months, and how the four huge Dutchmen who work on the vessel have dinner in the master's house.

'These men are great friends, but no-one can tell them apart. We just call them "the four

Dutchmen",' Pepen says, as he chews on the pink flesh of a fallen persimmon. 'Tonight they are bringing a friend. I heard Master say he's famous. A famous storyteller. From far away.' He spits out a seed and frowns. 'I'd like to be a storyteller. I tell good stories, huh, Mina?'

—

Mina has helped wait table for several nights now, but she has only had to serve the master, seated at the head of the table, alone. The quietness of the dining room is usually punctuated by the rustle of her sarong, the tinkle of china and cutlery, the buzz of the cicadas hiding in the nocturnal garden. But tonight the whole house reverberates with the presence of the Dutchmen. The floors vibrate as they stomp by, the walls echo with their loud voices. The master plays music on his gramophone, and when Mina enters the living area with a plate of *lumpia*, the men are bellowing along with its heavy tune and strange words.

She lowers her gaze as they take the spring rolls from the proffered plate. Suddenly they are quiet and, glancing up, she sees they are staring at her, smiling, curious, as their yellow teeth sink into the *lumpia*'s crispy skin. She backs out of the room and the din picks up again.

Pepen helps her lay the table with platters of chicken, salads in peanut sauce, savoury pastries and pickled fruits. Pepen keeps the visitors' glasses of beer filled to the brim. And he's right. Mina finds it hard to tell the difference between the big, pink men from the cargo tramp. But their friend, the storyteller, is taller, slim. His hair is black and his moustache is as shiny as a polished whelk. He has the look of a garuda hawk, and when he speaks, his voice is hesitant, deliberate, until he drinks more of his clear draught that has the pungency of the substance Pepen cleans the windows with.

It's not long before Mina becomes aware that one of the Dutchmen, the fattest of the four, watches her as covetously as he'd pondered the syrupy coconut pancakes on the dessert platter. Somehow he finds out that she is the one who cooks the *konro*, so he makes a point of only eating the rib dish, the gravy slicking his lips. While the others pour more and more food into their wide mouths, and shout and joke with each other over a card game, the fat man continues to watch her. He wipes sweat from between his chins and smiles so that his blue eyes crinkle almost shut. His friends tease and nudge him and even though they speak in their own language she can tell they are taunting him about her. The garuda man's dark eyes peer at her as he scribbles in a little black notebook, and the master laughs too, but not as loudly. When no-one else is watching, she sees him frown.

—

The following morning the master calls her away from the kitchen where Ibu Tana is teaching her to cook yellow chicken. Mina's hands are stained with turmeric and the freshly sliced garlic stings the tiny fissures in her coarsened fingertips. Wiping her hands down her sarong, she finds the master seated on the verandah next to the fat Dutchman, who is even pinker than the night before. He's wiping the back of his neck with a red bandana. The master explains that the man, who he calls Captain Brees, wants to practise Malay with her. He says this will be beneficial for her too, as she can learn some Dutch. The master's pale eyes are blank. She cannot tell if he is pleased with her or not. He tells her to stay in his gardens, not to go beyond the gates.

She leads the way down the front stairs, and the timber steps shudder as the captain lumbers along behind her. She can't look at him, can't smile, feels her insides shrink in his presence. Her head is hot like when Ibu Tana opens the door of the ravenous oven and it whooshes its fiery breath around her ears. The captain clears his throat, but doesn't say anything. He wipes at the back of his neck again, mops at the perspiration dripping down his temples, across his red cheeks. Stroking the brazen, cerise petals of the orchids between his thumb and finger, she notices his chubby fingers tremble a little and she wonders if he feels as shy as she does.

He points up high at the jagged palm leaves.

'*Daun kelapa*,' she says, and then remains silent until he points out a hibiscus. '*Bunga raya.*'

'*Bunga raya*,' he repeats.

But his pronunciation is so strange and funny to her ear, she is soon giggling at him, covering her mouth with a cupped hand as she has been taught by her mother, and he laughs with her, so that his whole body shudders up and down with each gasp. Once their lesson is finished he presents her with a small rattan box. It's painted in a wash of jade green with a pattern of pink dots, and inside she finds sweet-smelling frangipani flowers. She's never owned anything so pretty. He says something to her which she can't understand, smiles, pats her arm.

The master sees the captain off and Mina returns to the kitchen. While Ibu Tana is engrossed in counting the fifteen eggs to go into the *lapas legit* cake, Mina hides the rattan box at the back of the shelf that holds her bedding. Not until everyone is asleep later that evening does she take the box out again and, hiding it under her *kebaya*, she carries it all the way down to the beach. She lifts the lid and places it carefully on the sand. The frangipani fragrance escapes on the sea air. This time she wades with confident steps into the waves, the box of flowers clamped against her chest. The water is as black as squid ink, as warm as tears. She hums the tune her mother used to murmur to her, *kerning naning kerning naning*, nonsense words, yet the melody is so soothing. She holds her hand in front of herself, rotating it at the wrist as she sings, watching the moonlight glimmer across her milky fingernails. She calls for the Ocean Queen. Only when she feels Nyai Loro's strong, smooth pull, feels the soft arms suckle at her damaged thighs, does Mina scatter the flowers upon the sparkling water.

—

A kingfisher cackles high in the branches, ruffling its turquoise wings, watching for stray pieces of meat. The afternoon sunlight dapples Mina's skin as she stands in the shade of a banyan tree. She has never been among so many people. They are gathered in a clearing near the beach; men, women and children load tables with platters of rice, curries and sweetmeats.

Ibu Tana shoves a basket of *bacang* in her hands and nods to the nearest table. 'Make yourself useful. Stop staring and help us carry the food the master has provided.'

Mina places the basket on a table next to a bowl of rambutan. Pepen squeezes her elbow. 'That's the elder who is putting on the feast.'

The *priyayi*, an old Javanese man, slight and as bent as a knob of ginger, quietly surveys the food. He is accosted by several people who take his hand in theirs, bow their heads low. Mina already knows from Pepen that everybody in town, every single villager, from the ragged field worker to the elegant batik artist, has been invited to celebrate the town elder's successful tea harvest. Only the very meanest of the Dutch masters have neglected to give their workers the night off.

By the time the stage is erected and the *gamelan* band is assembled, it is dark enough to light the lanterns, which lend a flickering glow to the festivities. The *priyayi*'s servants encourage everyone to eat, heaping mounds of food on swatches of banana leaf. Mostly the guests sit cross-legged on the ground to watch the performance, except for the *priyayi* and his family, resplendent in rich velvets and jewels, who are seated at a table with a white tablecloth. Mina skirts the pretty dancing girls and admires the sprigs of jasmine that speckle their coiffed hair and the flecks of gold in the green satin of their costumes. But it is the *wayang* puppets, hanging from the side of the stage, that draw her close. She has never seen anything like them before.

The miniature, glossy people are gorgeous and grotesque, each one different. This one has a red face, angry black eyes, white rabbit teeth. This one is a warrior, with a tin sword inserted in its stick hand. The princess wears a striped sarong, and a golden, peaked headdress. The prince has a crown, and his black eyebrows are bold, his nostrils coiled. Mina lifts her hand, wants to feel his sharp nose.

'You'd better not touch it,' Ajat says, grinning. He nods towards the puppeteer. 'The *dhalang* has his eyes on you.'

Mina smiles back at Ajat but drops her eyes. Every time she sees him now, whether it's fleetingly in the master's yard when she takes food to the stablehands, or on their swift trips to the Chinese store, she feels as if a band tightens around her chest.

'Let's get away from here,' he says. 'I can't stand how they look at us like we're children.'

She follows his gaze to where a Dutch family has joined the *priyayi* at his long table. A pallid man watches the dancers, and his thin lips smile as if observing an infant stumble over its first steps. His wife surveys the villagers with a benign air and puzzles over the proffered food, while their three young daughters droop with boredom.

'Come with me.'

Mina follows Ajat from the quivering circle of light, through the bushes to the edge of the beach. A murmur of music and voices drifts through the branches as they settle under a banyan tree.

'The *priyayi*'s servant gave me these to taste,' Ajat says, pressing a small package into her hands. The food is wrapped in smooth, neat rectangles of banana leaf. 'He called them *lemper*.'

She presses the green wrapping to her nose. It's fragrant, more interesting than the watery smell of the triangular beef *bacang* Ibu Tana has taught her to make. When she peels away one end, the moist rice leaves a residue on the banana leaf, on her fingertips. She licks the coconut milk from her skin and bites into the *lemper*. The chicken is sweet; the shredded coconut catches between her teeth.

'Delicious.'

Ajat presses his mouth to hers, seals in the sweetness, the wonder. He softly takes her lower lip between his lips, runs the tip of his tongue along hers. The band around her chest tightens until she can barely breathe. Falling back, Mina scrapes the heel of her hand against the tree trunk. The full moon shines on Ajat's cheekbones, lights his teeth.

'Do you want to return to the feast?' he asks.

She nods slowly, touches the tips of her fingers against her mouth. She wants to reach her hand out, feel for his lips too. Leaning against the tree, she pulls herself into a standing position. Her legs are weak, can barely hold her, like the time she had the fever.

By the time they find the others, the lamps are guttering, transforming the villagers into shadow puppets. It's not until they are all walking home to the master's house that Mina realises she still clutches the *lemper* wrapping in her fist.

—

The next morning Mina waits in the kitchen courtyard, dressed in her good *kebaya*. But it is not Ajat in the buggy today, it is Yati, the other boy from her village. She scrambles up onto the bench next to him. 'Where's Ajat?'

Yati makes a grunting noise. 'His father summoned him back to the village.'

'For how long?'

Yati frowns. His face is chubby, has a fat, flat nose. 'What do you want to know for?'

She shrugs, watches a greenfinch hop to a lower branch of the persimmon tree. 'I'm just surprised he's not here, that's all.'

The buggy rolls down the master's long drive, turns onto the main thoroughfare. Mina leans her knees to the side of the buggy, away from Yati.

'Ajat might never come back. Who knows?' the boy says, lightly slapping the reins against the pony's back. 'His father wasn't happy about him coming here anyway. Said he could only stay a year at the most.'

Dismay flushes Mina's skin. Ajat may never come back. Her heart already misses him, but she also feels a pinch of jealousy. If only she too could go back home. Go back to the people she knows, the ones she loves. If only she could return home with him — with Ajat. But he is the chief's son. He is worth something to the village. He will not be traded. She has been exchanged for rice, tobacco, maybe even a live chicken or goat. There will be no need to summon her home.

Yati pulls the buggy to a stop at the back of the Chinese store. 'Ibu Tana said you know what to do.'

She stares into his face, then glances away,

has to gather her scattered thoughts like they are wisps of papery garlic skin caught on the breeze.

Entering the dim shop, she smells the spices, familiar to her now, and the white smoke that rises from the incense stick in front of the crimson and gold Chinese altar. She closes her eyes for a moment, remembers she needs four cans of butter — the red tins that feature a picture of a grazing cow, not the ones with the blue and white label. And black cotton to mend Pepen's trousers. How her mother would marvel at Ibu Tana's sharp little needle — but thinking of her mother scorches Mina's chest.

Today there is only one girl serving, the shorter one, who has a thick fringe of hair across her broad forehead.

'May I have eight potatoes please,' asks Mina, placing the cans of butter on the counter. She wonders if her voice sounds as tight as her chest feels. 'And a pound of flour?'

As the girl shovels potatoes into the bag and weighs them, Mina thinks of Ajat's smooth skin, his strong hands. She wonders if she will ever see them again.

She looks down at the bag of potatoes the Chinese girl pushes across to her. She's given her the wrong type, the sweeter kind. The girl is already measuring out the flour, and Mina knows that if she asks her to exchange the potatoes she will become grumpy, but if she takes them home, Ibu Tana will scream at her. Sweat moistens her underarms.

'You swim with the the sea dragon at night-time,' the Chinese girl says to her, softly. Her dark, almond eyes peer at Mina as she shovels another spoonful of flour into the container.

Mina's face slackens. She glances around the store. They're alone. 'What do you mean?'

'You've been seen.' The girl plonks the container down, tilts her head. Her black fringe is oily with sweat, hangs in straight, narrow strips like the teeth of a comb.

Mina shakes her head slowly. 'No.' All thoughts of home, of Ajat, of her mother, skittle away. 'Who says?'

'Gok. He guards the store during the night. He said he's seen you creep down to the beach, that you swim with a dragon.'

Perspiration prickles Mina's upper lip, but she forces a smile to her mouth. 'No. No, that is not true.'

'But you do swim there at night-time?' the girl persists.

Mina tries for a friendly, casual tone. 'Only the once. It was a very hot night.'

'I knew it,' the girl says, her thick lips widening

into a smirk. 'He probably saw a dolphin or a mackerel or something, the idiot.'

'Yes, yes,' says Mina, light-headed with relief. 'That reminds me. I also need to buy a fish. Whole. To bake.'

The Chinese girl scoops up the fish net, and climbs her little ladder. Swishing the net back and forth, she eventually pulls out a grey fish, as waxy and sharp as flint. She slaps it down on a wooden board, holds it still with her left hand.

'You best be careful,' she says to Mina. 'Horrible things could happen to you if men like Gok know you're wandering around alone at night.' Taking a knife, its blade keen and narrow, she positions it above the fish's head. 'But it'll be even worse for you if the local people think you're a witch.' She pierces the squirming fish above the gills, slices down through its throat until it's decapitated.

—

The sky has darkened, and cool drops of rain splatter her arms, her head, as they fill the cart with the goods. The sun has taken on the silver of the moon, the clouds are as leaden as her thoughts. Mina has lost her friend, Ajat, and she misses her mother. She is so heavy with sadness she can barely pull herself up into the buggy. She thinks of how she will also have to give up her evening visits to the sea, to the Ocean Queen.

The rash on her thighs rubs against her sarong as the buggy trundles home and the raindrops become plump and heavy, until the downpour drenches her hair, soaks through her *kebaya*.

—

Seven weeks pass and Ajat still does not return from the village. It rains every day. The driveway and roads are reduced to mud, and the master's lawn grows so tall it looks like a rice paddy. When she can escape her chores, Mina steps through his gardens, lets her feet sink into the cool rainwater, the mire of dark soil and grass. The earth is so drenched she sometimes sees worms wriggle blindly across the ground. She lifts her face to the sky, closes her eyes, and tries to feel each raindrop, each dash against her cheek, her forehead. It is in these moments, against the lit backdrop of her eyelids, that she pictures her mother by the fire, the black birthmark under her thumbnail as she guts the fish.

The only relief she feels from her loneliness is on days like today, when the cheerful captain visits her. In her time in the master's house she has learnt many Dutch words, but the captain still likes to visit her for their lessons. The master has told her to wait on the verandah, to sit on one of his cane chairs. She has seen the captain twice since that first language lesson, and each time he has presented her with a new gift from his travels. The batik from Malacca, with pink flowers and blue butterflies, she folded up tightly, and hid away in her rattan box. She was going to wear it one day for Ajat, but now she thinks she might give it to her mother. The second time the captain visited her, he gave her a whole jackfruit from Batavia. She hid it in a coal bag under the house and it had taken her and Pepen two days to feast on its sweet, pungent seeds.

She hears Captain Brees long before she sees him: his bellows to the master from his buggy, his stomps up the front staircase, the creaking of the floorboards under his tread. Taking a seat next to hers, he beams at her as he wipes his brow. He is so bulky that triangles of fat push through the pattern of the cane chair.

He hands Mina a sheaf of paper, a little like the newspaper the master reads. But rather than just lines of black figures there are pictures awash in colour.

'*Tijdschrift*,' he says loudly.

She inspects the paper, how it is folded down

the middle, how there are portraits of fair women on most of the pages. Tall women, who lean and taper like the dedalu tree. 'Tij-sift,' she says.

He laughs and shouts something at her, makes her repeat the word. She turns the pages, studies the long gowns, of dull green and blue. The fabric is plain, without the elaborate designs which decorate the very best batik. She rests her finger on an olive frock, says the word *pakaian*. He copies her, then tells her the word in his language, which she already knows, but obediently repeats. Turning the page, she studies their hats. '*Topi*,' she murmurs. They are much the same as those worn by the local Dutch ladies — short brimmed with a sprig of flowers on the side — but she is curious as to why one of the women has a dead lemur flopped over her arm. When she points, raises her eyebrows, the captain chuckles and speaks too swiftly for her. His words roll from his mouth like he is eating something hot, like he is choking on it. He embraces himself and pretends to tremble. Mina nods. She doesn't understand.

They peruse the magazine together, trading words, until she turns the last page. They smile at each other. He pats the pockets of his jacket, then his shirt, until finally he pulls forth a small basket, the size of a dumpling, from his breast pocket. He hands it to her.

Mina lifts the top and resting on a cloud of cotton lies a sparkling sliver of gold. Nobody in her village owns gold. She has never even touched it before. She'd only ever seen it jingle on the arms and ears of the Chinese merchant's daughters.

She carefully picks up the slender chain and even in the shadows of the verandah it glimmers. A bell encased in a tiny, golden ball tinkles as the chain sways, and Captain Brees laughs. She folds the chain over her wrist but it is too long, so the captain takes it from her, gestures to her feet. Lifting her left leg slightly, she watches as he leans down, his belly between his thighs, grunting with the exertion. He clasps the chain around her ankle, manages to fasten the tiny hook with his meaty fingers.

Mina thanks him profusely and holds her prayer hands to her forehead. When he takes his leave, she does not stand up. She feels too self-conscious, like the anklet has tethered her to the floor. But finally, of course, some time after he has said goodbye to the master, she has to move. She has to resume shredding the coconut for the master's curry.

The anklet feels very strange, nestled against the top of her foot. She cannot stop marvelling at it, fascinated with how special she has become. Every few steps, she stops to gaze down upon it, and is sure the strangeness of it makes her walk differently, more stiffly.

Mina creeps past the kitchen staff and slips into the back room. She takes out her rattan box and retrieves the piece of banana leaf that once wrapped the *lemper* she shared with Ajat. She presses the shiny leaf to her nose, inhales the coconut fragrance, and feels giddy, wobbly, like when she stands up in her father's fishing boat. That kiss. That kiss had opened up something in her. Smouldered through her limbs, heated her belly. She felt like she was bursting through her skin, like the lush, buttery flesh that peeks through the spiky crevices of an overripe durian. Placing the leaf back alongside the sarong from Malacca, she gazes down at the gold chain around her ankle. She decides she will keep it on, after all. She will not hide it.

When Ibu Tana sees the anklet she glares at Mina, but for some reason she leaves her alone. Mina doesn't understand it, but Ibu Tana no longer shouts at her or pushes her around. She doesn't yell when Mina brings the wrong produce back from the store, or when she overcooks the pork. In fact, Ibu Tana barely speaks to her. She uses Pepen to relay her messages.

'Ibu Tana wants you to take some fruit to the master's friend,' says Pepen.

Mina looks up from the peanuts she is shelling. Pops one in her mouth. 'Why do I have to go? Can't she just send Yati?'

'The master wants you to cook some *bubur* while you are there,' says Pepen. 'They're all sick. Even the servant.'

Mina pulls a face but places the basket of peanuts on the kitchen bench. 'Where is it?' She ties two cups of rice into a square of linen.

'Far away. You're going in the cart.' He takes a plucked chicken from the pantry, holds it out to her. 'Ibu Tana said to take this. She'll have another one killed for dinner.'

Mina walks down the kitchen steps carrying two baskets of food, and waits for the buggy. It hasn't rained for three days, and the sun, frangipani yellow, gently seeks out moisture from under the fallen leaves.

She looks up at the rumble of the cart's wheels, and wonders if it is a trick of the sun's haze and her secret thoughts that she sees Ajat seated on the driver's bench. But it is him. He's grinning down at her.

It's as if a canary is trilling high notes in her chest as she climbs onto the bench beside him. Its feathers prick and flutter, almost smother her.

'You're back,' she says. His full lips, his white teeth.

'Yes.' Ajat clicks his tongue to urge the pony onward.

'How is the village?' His chest is broader than she remembers. Bronzed.

He shrugs. 'The same. I had to go back and help my father. He wanted to plan some things.'

She's quick to realise what he means. A future. Ajat's future in the village. Something she would do anything to be a part of.

'And my mother? Did you see her? Or my father?'

He nods. 'Yes. Your mother has sent some smoked fish for you. She is sure you must be missing it.'

They smile at each other. She is so happy and so sad she could cry. But she won't. She hugs the feeling to herself and tells him what he has missed at the master's house: how Ibu Tana caught one of the gardeners pissing on the slices of mango left out in the sunlight to dry; the geese who wandered into the gardens and bit Pepen; the master's yen for juice made from custard fruit.

Suddenly she remembers the anklet, feels the weight of it. The buggy bumps over a rock and she can hear the faintest tinkle from its bell. She looks up at Ajat, at his fine, angular jaw and his ear, as neat as a seashell. She won't tell him of the captain's gifts.

—

The master's friend lives on the outskirts of town. The small hillside house has the sloped roof of the local *kampung* homes and is perched on stilts. A servant girl opens the door, ushers her in. Ajat is not far behind with the baskets of meat and fruit. There's a rancid smell to the house, of unwashed sheets and the seepage of illness. They tiptoe past one of the bedrooms, glimpse a man, as naked and pink as a swine, feverishly tossing in his bed. Mina looks away, holds her breath until they reach the back of the house where the kitchen is. The stovetop is simple, a grate over a fireplace, not much better than her mother's cooking arrangement in the village.

Ajat leaves the baskets on the table, returns to the pony. There's only the one tiny window in the kitchen and, peering through its grimy glass, Mina can't see where he is waiting. She fidgets impatiently at every little chore she has to do that long day, from boiling the rice to dismembering the chicken. First, though, she has to wash the dishes, encrusted in ancient food scraps, because the dratted servant, the only one in this sorry household, pretends to be ill, moaning as she rests her head in her arms. But Mina doesn't believe her, thinks her skin looks cool, her eyes clear, so she pinches her on the elbow, tells her to fetch some water, slice the pineapple. While the servant girl is gone from the room, Mina crouches down, unhooks the gold chain from her ankle. She wraps it in the linen that held the rice, screws it up, shoves it at the bottom of the fruit basket.

Finally, the rice in the *bubur* is soft, porridge-like, ready to ladle into bowls. Mina tells the servant girl that once it is cool she is to serve small mouthfuls to her master. She then escapes into the fresh air. She swings the baskets as she walks to the buggy, and smiles up at Ajat.

'That was a horrible place.' He grimaces as she joins him in the buggy.

She nods, widens her eyes. 'Horrible.' She catches a length of her hair to her nose, sniffs it. 'I hope I don't smell of it.'

Ajat takes her hair from her hands, smells it. 'Mmm. Still nice.'

His face is close to hers, and she feels shy as she remembers the last time they were alone. That night by the beach. She withdraws slightly, is quiet as the pony pulls them down the mountainside towards home. The ocean is spread out before them, framed by the curving coastline and a canopy of jagged banana fronds and coconut palms. The sun's glare bleeds into the horizon, has the shimmer of a coral trout. Ajat pulls the buggy into a clearing, and points at a low-set table.

'Let's watch the sunset from here. It won't take too long.'

She kneels, while he sits cross-legged. He places two pieces of fruit on the table. Both are round, smaller than apples, and encased in a hard skin that is darker than the master's mahogany blanket box.

'Mangosteen,' Ajat says. 'Have you ever tried one?'

She shakes her head. The Dutchmen had brought the master a box of them, and they filled a large bowl in the dining room, but not knowing what they were, she had yet to taste one. 'Did you take them from the basket of fruit?'

'Yes, but don't worry, Mina,' he says. 'They won't miss them. The master will never know.'

Mina hopes he's right. She presses its leathery skin. There is a cap of four fat leaves on its top, and a tiny, barky flower pressed into its base. 'How do I eat it?'

Ajat picks up the other one, squeezes and twists until the mangosteen lifts open, revealing five creamy white segments of fruit. He offers it to her, gestures for her to eat. She sniffs but there is no fragrance. She pokes her fingertip in, but can't peel a segment free, so she holds it to her mouth, flickers her tongue against its flesh. It's sweet, fresh, so she digs her tongue in, prises a piece of the mangosteen into her mouth, and its juice dribbles down her chin. The flesh is softer than a rambutan's, and encases a pulpy pip. She eats another piece, savouring the sour flavour that peeps through the sticky sweetness. Offering the last few segments to Ajat, she watches as he slurps up the fruit.

'There were five sections in this mangosteen,' he says. 'How many do you think are in this one?' He holds up the remaining fruit.

She's puzzled. It looks like it might be slightly smaller than the one they've eaten. 'Four?'

'Four?' His lips curl into a grin. 'Should we bet on it? I think there might be seven sections.'

'Okay.' She smiles back. 'But I've changed my mind. I think there are six.'

'But what shall we bet?'

Mina frowns. 'What do you mean?'

'Well, we have to bet something. If I win, then I get something, and if you win, then you get something.' His eyes seem darker than usual.

'Like what?'

Ajat looks to the sky for a moment. 'If I'm right, and there are seven pieces of fruit inside this mangosteen, then you have to meet me under the ebony tree tonight after everyone has gone to bed.'

Mina draws her hands to herself, presses them into her lap. 'You're mad.'

He laughs. 'No. And anyway, I have to give you the fish from your mother. So, if there are seven pieces you have to meet me. But if there are only six pieces, then you don't have to meet me. How's that?'

She's unsure, so she says nothing, watches as he twists open the mangosteen. He places one half in front of her. Her eyes count the plump segments. An empty roar is in her head like when she presses the opening of a cowrie shell to her ear, but she still manages to hear Ajat murmur, 'Seven.'

—

Mina can barely swallow her dinner that night. She scrapes the rice and chicken to the side of her plate, hides it under a cabbage leaf. All the evening noises — the clink of cutlery against china, the swishing of water in the washing bucket — clamour in her ears, irritate her senses, like an itchy blanket has been thrown about her shoulders that she wants to twitch away. She wishes they'd hurry up and go to bed. It's only when she notices Pepen wiping out the basket she'd used that day that she remembers her gold chain is still poked down into its recesses. She taps his hand aside, pulls out the twist of linen. She goes into the storeroom, Pepen following, and as she lifts the lid of her rattan box and slides the chain into it, he tells her a long story about the time the tooth doctor came and pulled a blackened molar from the master's mouth. He describes the splash of blood in the dish, and the rotten stench that was like the sediment of the stables on a wet day. He even mimics the master's moan, deep and drawn out, eyes squeezed shut.

Mina elbows him out of the way and gathers the eggs and vegetables she'll need for the morning. She rolls her eyes to the ceiling when Ibu Tana gives the other kitchen maids extra silver to shine.

Finally, they settle on their mats. Mina lies rigid, eyes pressed shut, and waits for their breathing to even out, slow down. Only when she hears the maids' faint snoring and a juddering fart leave Ibu Tana's lumpy stomach does she quietly lift her mat and pull it out onto the verandah. If anyone wakes, she will tell them she's moving outside where it's cooler.

The sky is luminous grey, the moon as slight as a pinbone. She gazes out across the shadows of the garden, to the very back where she knows the stables are. But it is too dark; no lights glimmer through the shroud of trees. Taking three cautious steps down the stairs, she cranes around to look at the silhouette of the ebony tree in the furthest corner of the garden. Ajat had pointed it out to her when he dropped her off — the tallest tree, the one past the chicken coops. She runs down the last few stairs lightly, flits across the grass, until she reaches the soka shrubs at the bottom of the garden. She hesistates, peering into the gloom that the moonlight cannot reach.

Ajat catches her around the waist. She has to cover her mouth with her hand to stop from squealing, from calling out loud, but the laughter that racks her body vibrates against his chest. He holds her close. Waits for her to calm. He makes soothing sounds against her ear, like she is one of the ponies. But she is trembling, wonders if she can ever be still again.

He leads her towards the tree's black trunk, hands her a straw bag. She loosens its tie, can already smell the smoked catfish her mother has sent her. Reaching in, she breaks off a little of the papaya leaf that encases the fish, nibbles on it, hopes its bitterness will steady her heartbeat. She offers the bag to him. 'Take some.' But he shakes his head, leans forward, folds her lips in his.

She sways against him, feels her knees weaken. He smells of the ocean again, of salt, of sandalwood. Her head falls back, heavy, and she stares at the glowing sky, at the glittering stars. She wants to stay like this, let the contentment seep into her bones. She only rights herself again when he steps back, drops his hands to his waist.

Unravelling his sarong, he pulls it from his hips and even though it is so dark that his body is a shadow, she looks away. He spreads the sarong on the ground, says, 'Lie down, Mina.'

She sits, waits for him to join her. He kneels down, wipes the hair from her face and his lips find hers again. He gently pushes her back. He hovers over her and his hand slides under her sarong. His fingertips trail along the inside of her thigh, but she holds his hand away from the rash. It hasn't flared in weeks, maybe because of the ointment the master gave her, of coconut oil and something else that has the odour of a goat's hide. She's afraid Ajat might feel the coarse skin, might sense it, and then he won't like her anymore. But he perseveres, and the sweep of his hand becomes soothing, as if she might melt away like butter in a frypan.

He lowers himself on top of her, pressing her into the ground. Twigs and grass prickle against her back through the thin fabric of the sarong. He's as hard as a pestle as he nudges between her legs, snuffles against her throat. She grips his shoulders as he pushes against her. Finally, he stabs into her, groaning, and it hurts, like she is being scaled, as he inches further inside. She presses the heels of her palms against her closed eyelids. She is his now, they are one. She wants to stay suspended in this moment because it feels good, she feels sated, but it's painful too. Opening her eyes, she is momentarily blinded by the pressure her palms have put on them, only sees gleaming light, but soon realises the glare is concentrated to one area, a few metres to their left.

The master holds a lantern aloft. 'Get off her,' he says, his voice guttural. His face is waxen, as rigid as his words.

Pepen stands just behind, both hands clamped across his mouth.

—

'I am sorry, Mina,' says Pepen. His big ears burn red, his eyes have the glaze of tears.

Mina turns her shoulder to him. She never wants to see his silly face again.

She's hiding in the small back room, leaning against the shelf that holds her things. She can hear Ibu Tana bang a fry pan onto the stovetop, crack three breakfast eggs into it.

Pepen twists his face around so he's in her line of sight, but she closes her eyes.

'I saw him grab you in the dark,' Pepen whispers. He glances over his shoulder, falls silent as one of the kitchen maids passes the doorway. 'I thought he was going to hurt you.'

She shrugs his hand from her arm. 'Just go away, Pepen.'

He stands next to her and sniffles. When she hears him leave she opens her eyes again.

Mina grips the shelf, watches her fingertips turn white, then bumps her forehead twice against the back of her hands. Does Ibu Tana know? Embarrassment curls through her stomach, breathes heat into her face. She thinks of the dry blood on her inner thighs, the leaden feeling between her legs. And she's sore, feels scalded like when she burnt the side of her thumb on the baking tray.

'Where is that fish girl when you need her?' Ibu Tana says from the kitchen.

Mina straightens up. As she approaches the cook, she squares her shoulders and wills her face to be as still as the teak Balinese mask that hangs in the master's sitting room.

There's the usual irritation on Ibu Tana's face, but that is all. 'Take the *perkedel* to the master before they get cold,' she snaps, pushing a platter towards her.

Mina steps closer to the table, but doesn't pick

up the platter. 'I don't feel well today. Can you get Pepen to do it?'

'No.' She slices through a papaya. 'That stupid boy has disappeared, so you will just have to get on with it.'

Mina's heartbeat drums loudly in her chest as she thinks of meeting with the master again. He will send her home. And, one way or another, the dishonour of it will kill her. She wants to see Ajat first. She must return to the village on his arm before the master has the chance to send her home in disgrace.

She takes up the platter, treads softly towards the dining room and peeps around the door. The room is empty. The master calls out from the verandah and she flinches. The patties slide across the plate. But he's shouting to one of the gardeners, not to her. She slips the platter onto the table, steps quickly back to the kitchen.

She has to return to the dining room twice more, with a basket of bread rolls and a pot of coffee, but it is not until her third trip with a bowl of fruit that she finds the master at the table. She comes to a halt in the doorway, studies how he pours the dark coffee, stirs in the sticky, sweet milk. She moves forward, places the bowl on the table as quietly as she can. Should she apologise? Should she cry? Worse — should she tell him she did not understand what had happened the night before?

The master flips open his newspaper, and his pale eyes flick across the pages. Apart from twisting slightly in his chair so that his back is to her, he shows no interest in Mina's presence.

—

It's not until late in the morning that she can escape her kitchen chores. While Ibu Tana is preoccupied with paying the vendor for the stove wood, Mina leaves the mortar full of crushed peanuts on the table and trips down the stairs, runs across the grass to the stables. She needs to talk to Ajat. She needs him to help her before the master changes his mind: tells everyone of her shame.

She rushes from one shed to the other, but they are empty of both ponies and men. The manure on the floor of the second shed is still fresh. Straw is strewn across the dirt. Mina walks behind the sheds, gazes across the fence into the neighbouring field, but all she can see are two water buffalo, ankle deep in the mud of the rice paddy, grazing on reeds.

'Are you looking for someone?' Yati comes up behind her, carrying a shovel.

'I'm looking for Ajat,' she says.

'He left at dawn.'

'Left?' she repeats, her voice rising in panic. 'Left for where?'

'He went home. To the village.' Yati frowns. Shaking his head, he enters the shed, starts scraping up clumps of manure.

Mina follows him, cups her hands over her nose and mouth in shock. 'Did the master send him away?'

Yati looks puzzled. 'No. He was only here for the one night. He's getting married. He came to town to swap two baskets of fish for oxen meat and nutmeg for the wedding banquet.'

The words pound over her like an icy wave. She almost staggers.

Turning back to the house, she holds her hands before her as if she is blind, conscious of every twig and dry leaf that catches under her toes. Parrots shriek high in the palms, the sunlight is too bright. Her fingertips tingle as she reaches forward.

Pausing, she looks back over her shoulder. 'Who will he marry?'

'Hamida.'

Hamida. An older girl from their village. Bossy, loud.

Mina wonders if Hamida has also felt the grass

prickle her back through the thin fabric of Ajat's sarong. She thinks not.

—

The other servants peek at Mina as she peels the bananas for the *pisang epe*. She knows her eyes are red, as puffy as a pastel. She'd wept in the servants' bathroom through the lunch hour into the afternoon. When others were in need of the *mandi*, she'd cried out that she had terrible cramps, that she could not move.

'I must have rubbed some sort of nettle in my eyes when I was picking the lemongrass,' she grumbles to them, dipping the banana in the batter.

Yati's words pulse through her. When the hot oil splutters and stings the back of her hand, she rubs the spot with her thumb. Ajat's getting married. As she tosses food scraps to the chickens, watches them peck at the grains of rice, quarrel over spinach stalks. Wedding feast. Meat and spices for the wedding feast. She lights the candles on the dining room table and they barely flicker in the still, humid air. Hamida. Tall and buxom. Lives in the village with her widowed mother. Mina passes her finger through a candle's tiny flame several times, then allows it to hover there for a moment, waits for the flame's bite. Hamida. Ajat.

Anger sears her chest, molten as simmering chilli sambal. By the end of the evening the rash on her thighs flares, and she drags her fingernails over the papery skin, glad of the streak of pain that momentarily masks her misery.

She shuts herself in the *mandi* again, smothers the rash in the ointment. Sobbing with relief, she stares at the white cream smeared across her legs as it douses the pain. She clutches the bottle to her chest, and scoops out a glob with her fingers, forces it into her mouth, to the back of her tongue. She swallows, but feels the ointment's slow glide down her throat, can taste where the gamey oil of the ointment pastes the insides of her mouth. She waits. She wants the cream to cool the fury in her chest, like it has calmed the sores on her thighs. But it rises in her throat. Clamping her hand to her mouth, she lurches outside, vomits into the undergrowth beneath the persimmon trees, where it glows against the fallen leaves.

Wiping watering eyes with the back of her hand, Mina crawls up the patio stairs to the kitchen. She doesn't care how much noise she makes as she steps over the sleeping kitchen staff and reaches for her rattan box. The gold chain tinkles as she lifts it from between the folds of the batik and clasps it back around her ankle.

—

Ibu Tana kneads the dough into the timber tabletop. 'The master doesn't want you tending table anymore.'

Mina searches the cook's face for malice but there's only a frowning curiosity in her beady eyes. Mina shrugs, keeps chopping the spring onions, but wonders if a blush eddies across her chest, creeps its sneaky fingers up her neck.

'I don't know what's been happening around here lately, but you and Pepen better get organised or else I'll have to hire a new kitchen maid,' she warns Mina, shoving the tray of bread in the oven. 'The stupid boy forgot to wipe the mud from the master's shoes last night and the fishcakes you cooked this morning were almost inedible.'

When Mina thinks of how the master and Pepen caught them under the ebony tree, she wants to curl up into herself like a scaly anteater. For days, Pepen has been cringing around her, trying to lure her back into friendship by taking on some of her chores. He told her stories of dark men from far away who wore turbans and purple scarves who had visited the master, of the time a rabid monkey chased Junius out of the forest. She was too distracted to pay him attention, though. It was only when he gave her his precious *kris* to cut back the chilli bush, and said, 'You should keep it. You need it more than me,' that he finally came into focus. His constricted voice, the way he blinked into the distance, belied the nonchalance of his words. She squeezed his thin hand, smiled, and returned the dagger to him.

But still, a hardness suffuses her chest, burdens her shoulders, makes her feel heavy. It is only late one night, when she lies on her mat and remembers the time her mother fed her a clove syrup for a sick stomach, of how she stroked the tears back from Mina's face with the flat of her free hand, that the hardness in Mina thaws, and a tear trickles down the side of her face, teeters over her right ear. She squashes the tear into her skin with her fingers, rises from the bedding and walks out to the verandah.

In vain, her eyes search beyond the other houses and palm trees for a glimpse of the sea. She will run away. She will flee to the water's edge and the Ocean Queen will tell her what to do. And if something happens to her — if that sly guard sees her, or if a villager thinks she's a witch — who cares, after all?

In the kitchen, one of the maids turns over,

says something in her sleep. Mina decides that tomorrow she will pack her few posssesions. She will escape.

—

'Mina, the master wants you. On the verandah,' says Pepen. Mina is surprised, but as she brushes past, he catches her arm. 'He's with the captain.'

She steps lightly through the house, can almost feel her heavy mood dissipate as the morning mists lift from the mountaintop. Finally, someone who will be pleased to see her.

The two men stand at the top of the front stairs. The master scrutinises his fingernails as she approaches, but the captain seems nervous. Sweat drips down his reddened cheeks.

'The captain has asked my permission for you to accompany him on his next voyage,' the master says swiftly in Malay. He smiles but his pale eyes are cold. 'I have told him that you may.'

Disbelief pricks the skin on the back of her neck. The master is giving her away. Alarm makes her insides shrink, but the lonely rage that has kept her company for weeks keeps her gaze steady.

The captain looks from the master to her. Although he can't quite understand the master's words, there's a hopeful smile on his fat face as he nods at her.

Mina's smile to the captain is fixed as she leads him down the stairs towards a garden setting by the coffea shrubs.

She kneels on the grass next to his garden chair and he beckons to her, then lifts her onto his lap. His huge belly is surprisingly firm. She teeters on his legs, holding her hands tightly together, crossing her ankles. He calls her *schatje*, his treasure, as he struggles to retrieve a small booklet from his breast pocket. Taking out two photographs, he shows her the first one, a portrait of the place from which these large Dutchmen come. The master has many such photos and paintings in his bedroom and sitting room. In this picture, there is a road of flattened stones and a very long house. She traces her finger along it, says, 'big house', and the captain laughs and explains to her that it is actually a row of connected, narrow dwellings. And everything is grey. Even the light looks grey. The captain points to one of the houses and then points to himself. She nods and peers at the picture again, but there isn't much else to see.

The next photo is of two women; his mother and sister, he tells her. She studies this photo more closely. These women do not look like Captain Brees at all. They are very thin and wear dark gowns that are buttoned high on their necks and flow low to the floor. Their hands are folded before them and their ashen faces are grim. The captain tells her he will take her to this grey place, where the rain falls white and solid and the women cover their whole bodies from the cold air and stares of men. He says they will visit Singapore and eat *rijstafel* at the Van Dorth Hotel and shop for her first pair of shoes. As he says this, he picks up Mina's foot, so small and brown in his large, meaty hand, and chuckles at the gold anklet. He asks her again if she will go away with him when they leave port. Mina thinks of the master's house, of how only Pepen will speak to her. And she thinks of how she can't get home to the fishing village. She presses her prayer hands to her forehead and thanks the captain. She nods yes.

—

When she hears that Mina will leave with the captain in the morning, Ibu Tana places the heavy knife onto the tabletop and presses her eyes shut. 'Ah,' she exhales. 'Now I understand why the master no longer prefers you.' She looks Mina up and down. 'What have you been up to, you shrew?'

Mina is helping Pepen fold the tablecloths. She avoids eye contact as she smooths the creases from the fabric. 'Nothing. The captain's just a very kind man.'

A snort whistles from Ibu Tana's nostrils. 'He won't marry you, you know. You will be nothing better than a *pelacur*.'

Mina's head rears back as she glares at the old cook — that toady, terrible woman. *Pelacur*? Mina wasn't like one of those poor, shunned women who eked out a dreary existence down by the wharf. She didn't wander the dirt roads heavy with child, bereft of a future. But she knows exactly what the captain wants of her, whether they marry or not. She thinks of the darkness of that night, of her body sinking into the ground under the weight of Ajat. Of how she thought that meant they were one, that they would be interwoven forever. She's almost thankful this is no longer a mystery to her. Almost.

'You don't know what the captain will do.' Mina's words are as inflexible as a cleaver. 'Whatever it is, it will be better than living here with you.'

She drops the tablecloth into a basket and, ignoring the leg of goat Ibu Tana has laid out on the kitchen table for her to dice, makes her way down to the stables.

'Yati, when you are next in the village, can you tell my parents I've gone away to be married?'

Yati straightens up from where he's scraping the pony's hoof. 'Who are you marrying?'

'It doesn't matter. Just tell them I will be fine. I am happy.'

She holds her chin high, but her smile falters as she thinks of what she will miss. She wishes she could have a wedding at home, with fragrant *sedap malam* petals entwined in her hair, and the sacred, embroidered matrimonial batik swathed around her hips and over her shoulder. Her mother would cook her favourite snapper *pepes* sprinkled with salted anchovies and treacly sweet soy sauce. And her father would not fish that day. He would sit with Mina's husband on a rattan rug and sip rice wine.

'I will see them soon,' she says over her shoulder, as she moves back towards the house.

Mina thinks of how one day when she is a fine and rich lady, with a dark gown buttoned high on her neck, she will return from the grey place and buy her parents a proper house. They will leave their thatched hut and endless fish behind.

But not yet. She feels a dip in her stomach like she's falling from the tallest palm tree. She may not see her parents for a long time. Impossible to return now, with nothing, to a village where Ajat is married to Hamida. She will have to wait, as long as it takes for the spiny stems of her heart to soften, until she can return with a full basket. Mina leans against a tree, rolls her forehead gently against the prickly bark. She takes a deep breath. She will need to be very strong. She will need to be like one of the *dhalang*'s *wayang* puppets, as hard as lacquer, as enduring.

The clouds are low the next morning when the captain comes to collect her. He and the master laugh loudly as they stroll through the gardens, but as the cart draws away, the master frowns.

Mina holds her rattan box in her lap. She lifts the lid so she can peek at the pheasant feather, sleek and the colour of ochre, that Pepen had pressed into her hand as a parting gift. His eyelashes were wet and a translucent trail of snot reached his upper lip as they walked down the back stairs. He rushed to finish telling her the story of the Javanese prince who constructed a thousand temples in only one night for his princess. 'That is love, true love, isn't it, Mina?'

She doesn't say goodbye to Ibu Tana who stands at the stove with her back to Mina, or to the kitchen maids, kneeling on the patio grinding spices like the very first time she'd seen them that day she arrived with Junius. She doesn't take one last look at the persimmon trees, or the ebony tree looming in the corner of the garden, and she doesn't breathe in the scent of the coffea flowers.

All through the East Indies they knew that the supercargo and the chief engineer had executed justice on the trollop who had caused the death of the two men they loved.

W. Somerset Maugham,
The Four Dutchmen

III

Mina clambers up the gangway of the tramp behind the captain. The vessel sways with the waves but not as fiercely as her father's small fishing boat when he guides it out to sea. Several sailors dash back and forth, readying the cargo and tramp for departure, while the captain's three friends are gathered together on the quarter-deck, shouting orders. They look serious. These must be their work faces, Mina decides. She smiles shyly at them, for these are the men who, on their noisy card nights at the master's, had tried to cajole her into sipping beer and teased her with songs of love. But as the captain introduces them — Bulle, the chief officer, darker than the others; Haas, the supercargo, who has a thin moustache; and the engineer, Jonckheer, the tallest — they continue to scowl, continue on with their work. As she passes, the engineer turns his head and spits on the deck.

The captain shows her his cabin, a poky space just big enough for a narrow bed against the outboard wall, with a desk tucked into the nearest corner. He bids her to sit on the mattress, places her rattan box in the small bookshelf that occupies the other corner of the cabin. Above the desk is a portrait of a couple; she thinks maybe it is another picture of the captain's mother. The woman stands just in front of a man who has the captain's thinning fair hair, his thick, gingery eyebrows.

The captain gestures to the upper deck. 'I work now.' He holds his hands in front of himself, palms flat to her. 'You wait.' He backs out, closes the door softly.

Mina kneels up on the lumpy mattress and peers out the porthole. The water is as blue as the hood of the fig bird, and she can just see the damp sand of the beach. It's not long before the drone of the tramp's engine pulsates through her body. She feels the pull of the ocean as they edge their way from port, but also a painful tug back towards what she knows. The sun has not reached its highest point, so her mother must still be slicing open the fish from the morning catch. Her father probably squats nearby, smoking. But there is no-one here to wave her off, no-one here who will miss her. She hops down from the bed, and inspects the captain's books to take her mind off the fading landscape of home.

—

Mina keeps mostly to the cabin during the first few days of the voyage. When the captain has finished his day's work and eaten with the other crew members, he joins her there. He shows her his collection of atlases; the coloured lands that have been discovered and named, and those that are still waiting to have their mark upon them. He draws a line from where they have just left, to the port in Nieuw Guinea where they will next dock.

He brings her fruit and rice dishes, fresh from the crew's *rijsttafel*. He laughs when she eats with her hand. He gives her a heavy silver spoon, and shows her how to dip its tapered end into the curry. The spoon is so large, she only covers a third of it with *nasi goreng*, and when she licks the rice from its surface, the silver leaves a metallic aftertaste in her mouth.

He flourishes a mangosteen in front of her. Mina stiffens, remembers her wager with Ajat. Ajat and Hamida.

'Look, *schatje*, see the brown flower at this end of the fruit?' His sausage finger daintily points it out for her. 'Count its petals. One-two-three-four-five.' He twists open the mangosteen, reveals five portions. His face lights up. 'Five,' he cries. But his brow lowers when he sees Mina's face tighten. 'You don't like my trick? It is no witchery, Mina. Everyone knows that if you count the petals you can tell how many pieces are inside.'

She pretends to laugh, claps her hands, but she won't eat any of the fruit.

—

Two evenings later Mina carries a jug of fresh water from the galley. The light from the saloon spills onto the deck. She knows supper time is almost finished, that the captain will be in his cabin soon, but she's curious to see where the men eat their meals, what they do when they're not working around the tramp.

As she draws close to the open doorway, she slides her back to the wall and steals closer to sneak a look into the saloon. She knows to stay hidden. Mostly the crew ignore her, although on the third day of the voyage Haas and Jonckheer had complained to the captain of her presence on the upper deck, called her 'that Malay girl'. And yesterday she'd heard Jonckheer mutter 'hussy' just before he hawked onto the deck floor. When she'd later asked the captain what he meant, the captain had stomped away, and she heard him shouting at the engineer down in the hold.

In the saloon, there's a long table, laden with the half-finished dishes of their *rijsttafel*. Several of the crew crowd one end of the table, talking, smoking over their empty plates. Their voices are raised to counter the scratchy music that blares from the gramophone in the corner of the room. They joke and peg screwed up pieces of paper at each other as they continue on with their gaming. At a separate table, a square table for four, the captain is seated with the chief officer, the supercargo and the engineer.

The captain stands, waves his hands as he smiles at the others, but they gesture for him to sit, call for him to take up his cards.

Bulle, the dark one, pours more beer into the glass in front of the captain. 'Stay, you old rascal, stay.'

'At least finish a game of *klaverjas*, for God's sake,' says Haas. His face is flushed, annoyed. He gulps down a whole tumbler of beer, and his head rolls as he pours more into his cup.

'No, no,' protests the captain, backing away from the table. 'I must check on my Mina.'

Bulle throws his cards on the table, takes a swig of his beer, but Haas's chair scrapes as he pushes himself to his feet, the table rattles as he slams his fist down on it. The room falls quiet, except for the gramophone that continues to scratch away.

'You are making a fool of yourself, you stupid man!' Haas shouts at the captain. He's unsteady on his feet as he tries to poke the captain in the chest. 'You should never have brought a woman on board. Never. This is no place . . .'

Mina grips the jug to her belly and runs back to the captain's cabin. When the captain joins her several minutes later, he looks glum. His brow is heavy, his fleshy jowls droop. He tells her how the others, his three friends, are annoyed with him. He pulls his face into a grimace to show their anger. They don't like him spending so much time with her, spoiling their fun, keeping him from late nights of beer and cards.

Mina rests her hand on his thick arm, feels the texture of the short, curly hairs that cover his skin.

He smiles sadly at her with his cod-blue eyes, embraces her close into his body. 'I just want to be with you.'

—

Early in the morning Mina climbs onto the upper deck so she can feel the sun on her shoulders. She glances around warily for Haas and Jonckheer, but has chosen this early hour because she knows from the habits of the captain that these Dutch sailors like to sleep off the excesses of the evening.

Mina takes a seat on a stool and opens up the small magazine she has brought from the captain's cabin. It's full of writing that she cannot read, but she likes the strips of curious pictures, drawings of people and animals on funny adventures. But the wind whips the pages back and forth. She closes it, holding it shut in her lap, and watches the dark water peak and glint. After a few minutes, she senses a shadow to her right. The chief officer, Bulle, stands a few metres away, arms crossed, staring at her. His lip lifts, like when a dog snarls, but she thinks it's a smile, so she smiles back, doesn't want to provoke him.

The day before, on her way to the galley with her used dishes, they had met each other in the narrow corridor. Instead of waiting, the chief officer pressed against her as he shuffled past. He was stinky; the stench of onion from his cavernous armpits, the pong of damp fishing nets wafted from his shoes. In her head, Mina calls him *Bau-Bau* Bulle: smelly.

But now Mina's smile snags as his eyes roam

slowly over her body, down her shoulders, across her outstretched legs. She turns away, lets her hair fan across half her face, tries to pretend he is not there.

—

It's late afternoon when they dock somewhere on the Nieuw Guinea coast, and the captain goes ashore with four other crewmen in order to deal with the local traders. He leaves Mina with Johan, the cook in charge of the galley.

Johan admires how deftly she fills the pastels with egg and noodles, how neatly she curls the edges of the pastry.

'You are well-trained,' he says, beaming at her. He speaks mostly in Dutch, but adds Malay words if he sees she doesn't understand. 'You must have had a good teacher.'

Mina grimaces and tells him of how Ibu Tana flicked water into her face if she didn't concentrate, and how red her knuckles could get when the cook swatted them with the ladle.

'My sweet, you're lucky you were not trained in Belanda.'

She looks across the table at him. 'You've been there?' She's keen to know of this place. She wants to know what to expect.

'Of course. I was born there,' he says, stirring the peanut sauce. 'My father was a Dutchman, but my mother was a little Indo woman from Makassar.'

Johan's skin has the sheen of amber, is lighter than hers, but his eyes are dark, almost as black as a coffee bean.

'From now on you must help me every day with the *rijsttafel* for the sailors,' he says. 'I'll teach you how to roast duck in banana leaves and how to make a *speculaas* cake so delicious, the crew will weep for home.'

—

The sun has set by the time Mina leaves the galley. The spices from the beef rendang infuse her hair, and her fingers are stained with coppery cinnamon. She leans over the side of the tramp, smells burning copra, can see smoke rise from among the coconut palms. The sky is the dull grey of a mackerel that has been dead for days.

She makes her way to the captain's cabin. She wants to wash before he returns. The only light in the darkened corridor comes from an open cabin: Bau-Bau's. She doesn't want him to see her, so she tries to squeeze past in the shadows, but as he's taking a swig from a bottle of dark liquor he glimpses her from the corner of his eye.

He snarl-smiles at her. Beckons. 'Come. Come,' he says. 'You like books. Look, I have many books.'

She doesn't want to appear rude, so she peers into his room from the corridor. He gestures towards three green, leather-bound books that are stacked on a wooden crate.

'Come in, come in,' he says, taking her elbow. 'You can see them in here.'

Alcohol is heavy on his breath. He stumbles back a step, pulling her with him. She doesn't resist. Bau-Bau doesn't grumble about her like Haas and Jonckheer do. She wants to appease him, humour him, thinks that maybe he will be her friend, like Johan.

He leans against the door as it clicks shut.

Mina learns that, really, he hates her as much — more — than the others do.

—

It is too late by the time the captain finds them. He knocks and pokes his head around the door, and the smile that lifts his heavy cheeks freezes. His eyes switch from the chief officer, naked and slick with perspiration, to Mina, who is huddled into the corner of the cabin, a sheet wrapped around her body. He gobbles at words that will not come, and lumbers from the room, staggers down the corridor.

When he returns, it is with his pistol, which he waves at Bulle, who's tying a sarong around his thick stomach.

Bulle sneers, takes another slug from his bottle. His words slur as he says, 'You would shoot me for a hussy such as this?'

The captain becomes red in the face, much redder than when he's laughing, takes a step back, and shoots the chief officer in the chest. He clasps the pistol to his own forehead as he watches the life gurgle and shudder its way from the chief officer's body.

Then his wild eyes find Mina, and she realises she is screaming and screaming. He aims the pistol at her.

She shields her head with her hands, crouches lower into the floor. 'No, no. Please. I didn't mean for it to happen. I didn't mean for it to happen.' But she's speaking in Malay; can't gather words together that he might comprehend.

The captain's hand wavers, and he lurches from the room again.

Several moments later the sound of another shot crashes through the silence.

Haas and Jonckheer stumble into the cabin, and their bulk fills the confined space. They fall to their knees, bellow over the body of their friend. They lift the chief officer like he's a small child, cradle him onto the bed.

They leave the cabin and a few moments later Mina hears them crying out again, further down the corridor. Mina's not sure how long she cowers in that corner. She presses her forehead into the wall, away from where Bau-Bau lies, away from where his right hand hangs limp over the edge of the bed. She wants to crawl across the floor, escape into the corridor, but she's unsure of what she will find there. Where is the captain?

The engine of the tramp stutters to life, and she feels the magnetic pull of the ocean as they leave port. If only she were at home with her mother, lying on her mat, listening to the waves and her mother's gentle breathing. If only Ajat had taken her — taken her home, taken her as a wife.

When Haas and Jonckheer return she immediately knows, from the hatred that skews their faces, that they have not come back for Bau-Bau, they have come back for her.

She tries to slip past Haas, almost reaches the doorway, but he grabs her by the hair. He braces her to his side as he unclasps his belt, loosens his trousers. Mina tries to push away from him, so breathless she cannot scream, and he slaps her hard across the face, so hard she falls to the floor.

There's a ringing in her ears when he drags her close, shoves himself into her. Her joints strain to fit his girth. She can smell the garlic on his breath, can see spinach caught between his front teeth. She covers her face with her hands, shrinks away from another blow to the head from his raised hand. She thinks this is how it will be for her now, and when the supercargo finishes, she waits for Jonckheer to thrust his way into the other's leavings. But he stays by the door, turns his head, spits on the floor.

Haas presses relentless fingers around Mina's throat, tries to push the life from her. She peels at his fingers, feels her eyes bulge with the force, tries to wriggle out of his hold.

Jonckheer takes Haas by the shoulder, says he has a better idea.

A feral stench of fear coats Mina's skin, reminds her of a tethered goat just before its throat is cut. They try to pick her up, but she screeches, digs her nails into their pink skin. Jonckheer punches her in the stomach, and she retches as he stuffs one of Bau-Bau's briny socks into her mouth, securing it with a bandana. They tie her hands and feet with rope, haul her up onto the upper deck. As they pass the galley she sees Johan's black eyes peeping through a crack in the door. She squeals for him through her gag as he disappears back into the galley, and the door gently closes.

It's pitiful how weak she is compared with the two men. She flaps on the deck like a fish. When she hears Haas call her a Malay trollop, her chest fills with so much hatred, she's sure the power of it will help her break free of her restraints. She wants to hurt these men, to sink her heel into their scrotums, to stomp on their fleshy throats. She yearns to kill them, these fat devil men. She wants to kill them.

But she can't.

When they lift her, she writhes in their strong hold, she bucks her legs, but they easily hoist her onto the side of the tramp and roll her into the dark sea.

—

The first shock of the cold ocean smites the fury from her. She falls through the water, as swiftly as a coin. Blackness smothers her, surrounds her in tiny bubbles. The blurred lights of the tramp waver and dim as she sinks. She panics, inhales salty water through her nostrils. A blank pressure builds inside her head. She feels she might burst.

Putri...

Her descent slows. Specks of seaweed and silt swirl around her head, punctuate the murky depths.

Putri... Princess...

The Ocean Queen whispers to her, wraps her warm arms around Mina's constricted body. Loosens the folds. Nyai Loro Kidul promises her much, buoys her descent.

Mina's head relaxes back and the tramp is nothing but a glowing spot in the distance.

The silken water draws Mina further down into nothingness.

Until she is finally back in the sunlight, scaling fish with her mother.

Acknowledgements

I would like to thank Seizure and Viva la Novella for this wonderful opportunity and, in particular, Alice Grundy, for her warm support and careful, insightful editing of my work.

Big thank you to the people in my writers' groups who helped me bring this novella to life: Laura Elvery, Emma Doolan, Kathy George, Andrea Baldwin, Trudie Murrell, Janaka Malwatta, Jonathan Hadwen, Catherine Baskerville, Chloe Callistemon and Rohan Jayasinghe. Love and gratitude to Ellen and David Paxton, Lesley Hawkes, Fiona Kearney, Gillian Paxton and Meg Boland (Mum) for your kind feedback. As always, thank you Jim Riwoe (Papa) for patiently answering my never-ending questions about Indonesia, and love to Elis, Dave, Bianca, Jett and Mae.

VIVA
LA NOVELLA

Viva la Novella is an annual prize awarded for short works between twenty and fifty thousand words. Since its beginnings in 2013 the award has published twelve short novels by twelve outstanding Australian writers.

For more information, please visit our website www.seizureonline.com

VIVA LA NOVELLA 2017 WINNERS

A Second Life by Stephen Wright
978-1-925589-04-7 (print) | 978-1-925589-05-4 (digital)

The Fish Girl by Mirandi Riwoe
978-1-925589-06-1 (print) | 978-1-925589-07-8 (digital)

VIVA LA NOVELLA 2016 WINNERS

Populate or Perish by George Haddad
978-1-925143-22-5 (print) | 978-1-925143-23-2 (digital)

The Bonobo's Dream by Rose Mulready
978-1-925143-24-9 (print) | 978-1-925143-25-6 (digital)

VIVA LA NOVELLA 2015 WINNERS

Welcome to Orphancorp by Marlee Jane Ward
978-1-921134-58-6 (print) | 978-1-921134-59-3 (digital)

Formaldehyde by Jane Rawson
978-1-921134-60-9 (print) | 978-1-921134-61-6 (digital)

The End of Seeing by Christy Collins
978-1-921134-62-3 (print) | 978-1-921134-63-0 (digital)

VIVA LA NOVELLA 2014 WINNERS

Sideshow by Nicole Smith
978-1-922057-97-6 (print) | 978-1-921134-24-1 (digital)

The Other Shore by Hoa Pham
978-1-922057-96-9 (print) | 978-1-921134-23-4 (digital)

The Neighbour by Julie Proudfoot
978-1-922057-98-3 (print) | 978-1-921134-25-8 (digital)

Blood and Bone by Daniel Davis Wood
978-1-922057-95-2 (print) | 978-1-921134-22-7 (digital)

VIVA LA NOVELLA 2013 WINNER

Midnight Blue and Endlessly Tall by Jane Jervis-Read
978 1 922057 44 0 (print) | 978-1-922057-43-3 (digital)

Available online and from discerning book retailers